# GEORGE THE BABYSITTER

GEORGE THE BABYSITTER

by Shirley Hughes

Copyright © 1975 by Shirley Hughes
under the title HELPERS, published by
The Bodley Head, London.

First American edition published 1977 by
Prentice-Hall, Inc., Englewood Cliffs,
New Jersey

Prentice-Hall, International, Inc., London
Prentice-Hall of Australia, Pty. Ltd.,
    North Sydney
Prentice-Hall of Canada, Ltd., Toronto
Prentice-Hall of India Private Ltd.,
    New Delhi
Prentice-Hall of Japan, Inc., Tokyo
Prentice-Hall of Southeast Asia Pte. Ltd.,
    Singapore

Printed in U.S.A.

Weekly Reader Children's Book Club presents

# GEORGE
# THE
# BABYSITTER

by

## Shirley Hughes

**Prentice-Hall, Inc., Englewood Cliffs, New Jersey**

Mike, Jenny and Baby Sue's mother goes to work during the day and George comes to babysit.

He looks after the children, and together they look after the house.

"Now," says George, "let's
clear the dishes from
the table and stack them on the sink."

Not one is broken. George helps. Mike helps.
Jenny helps. Everybody helps.

Except Sue, who's just a baby. She sits in her high chair, dropping her bread on the floor, a little bit at a time.

"Now let's straighten up here," says George in the bedroom. "The beds aren't made…

there are comics all over the floor…

and who's been walking about in muddy boots?"

But the toy cupboard is too full to put anything away.

George thinks that there would be a lot more room if they threw away some of these old broken toys.

Mike is a great help in carrying them out to the trash.

But Jenny thinks
it's a shame
to get rid of
so many old friends.

Luckily Sue has cleared an entire shelf of the
bookcase all by herself.

It's just right for Jenny's old toys.

Sue is very tired
from all that work,
so George puts her down

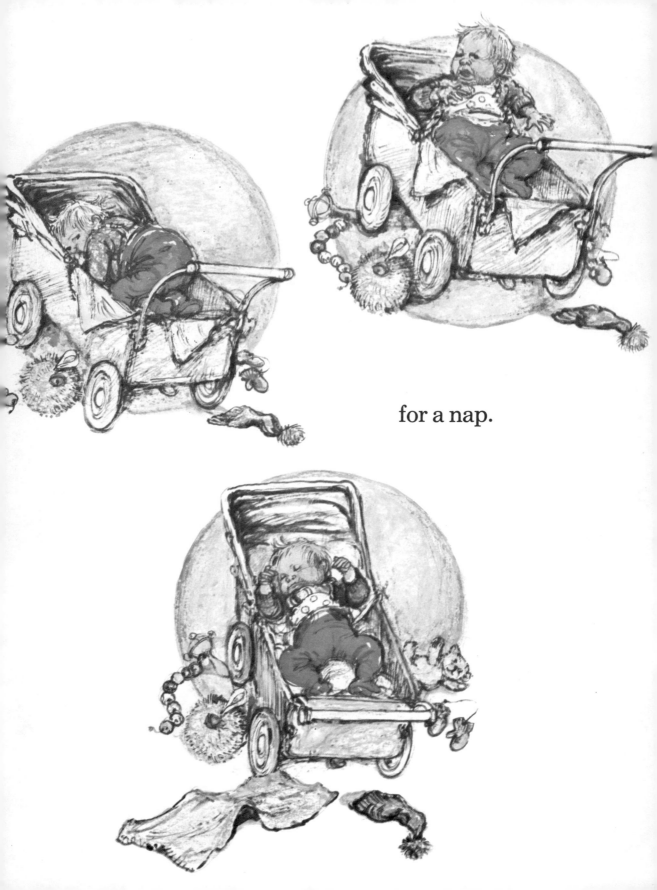

for a nap.

George takes Jenny and Mike outside.
"Perhaps we could do some weeding," says
George.

But Mike and Jenny aren't sure
which are the weeds and which
are the plants. Neither is George,
so they pick four flowers
for Mother when
she comes home.

It's time for lunch. Jenny thinks she can
remember how the knives, forks and spoons
go. George serves the soup and Mike helps Sue
with her chocolate pudding.

After lunch, when George sits down to read his magazine, the children play a game of boats with cushions. The shiny part of the floor is the sea and the carpet is the land.

Sue keeps getting out of her boat into the water. When there is a shipwreck, they have to climb up George to keep from being drowned.

George soon says crossly that he's had enough of this game, so they go out to the shop.

At the shop George buys some chewing gum
for himself and some candy for the children.

Sue sits outside chatting with her friends.

On the way home they stop at the playground.
George pushes Jenny very high on the swing.

When they get
home George thinks
he will finish off
painting the sitting
room window frame.
But this is not a
good idea.

They all watch television instead.

Suddenly George remembers that
none of the washing has been done.

Now Mike and Jenny do a really helpful
thing. They give Sue a bath all by themselves.
They make sure that the water isn't
too hot, and hold on tight while they soap
her all over. Afterwards they put on her nightie
and even remember to brush her hair.

There's someone at the door.
Mother's home!

Now it's time for the children to
have their supper and go to bed.

Mother says they've all been very good.

How could George have managed without
them?